Perkins The Halloween Cat

Words by

Liz Hedgecock

Pictures by

Lucy Shaw

WHITE
RHINO
BOOKS

For Henry, Abby, Frankie and Luna
and all future cats! – **L.H.**

ISBN-13: 979-8839616042

Once upon a time there was a very handsome cat called Perkins.

His fur was black as night,
his eyes were emerald green,
and his whiskers were long and twitchy.

People who met Perkins stroked him and said, 'He looks like a witch's cat.'

Perkins purred and felt very important.
'Perhaps I should try being a witch's cat,' he thought.

Perkins knew Halloween was coming; Mum had helped the children carve a pumpkin.

'I'm gonna be a vampire this Halloween, Perkins!' Jessica jumped up and down. 'Olly's gonna be a ghost! And we'll get lotsnlots of sweets!'

Perkins purred...

...and a plan formed in his brain.

One day the children rushed home from school. 'Calm down!' Mum said, laughing. 'Vampires don't giggle!'

Jessica ran downstairs wearing a cape and pointy fangs. Perkins was quite jealous. Then he heard someone bump into a door. 'I can't seeeeeeee!' wailed Olly.

'Hang on, I'll cut you some eyeholes,' said Mum. She went upstairs, and led Olly-in-a-sheet down.

'Come on, Mum!' The children picked up their treat pails and opened the front door.

Perkins looked outside. It was getting dark.
A blast of cold air made his fur stand on end.

'Mu-u-u-u-u-m!'

'I'm coming!'
Perkins heard
footsteps and
jangling keys.

'Bye, Perkins!'

But like a shadow, Perkins
had already slipped outside...

Perkins strolled along the pavement, looking for witches. 'Ooh, a black cat!' said a princess.

'Black cats are unlucky if they cross your path,' said the princess's mum. 'Time to go home.'

'I want to stroooooke him!' But the princess was towed away.

Perkins felt quite offended. Why would I be unlucky?' he thought.

More and more creatures walked along the road.
Perkins didn't see any witches, though.

Or any other cats.

'BOO!'

Someone jumped out at Perkins and he ran down a path. He turned, and saw a monster! With sharp teeth and a dangerous glint in its eye!

But it wasn't running after him.

It couldn't grab him, because it didn't have arms.

And the glint in its eyes looked just like the flame when Mum lit the pumpkin.

Perkins backed away hoping no one had seen him.

It was really dark and quiet.

Perkins walked along, eyes wide, ears up.
But nobody was there.

'Perhaps I should go home,' he thought.

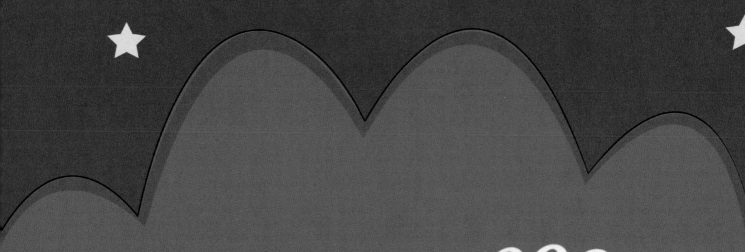

WOOOOOOAAAARGHHOOOOO!

Oh no! Ghosts! Three of them!

'WOOOOOOOOOO!'

The ghosts giggled and ran away.

Perkins watched them go.

'What strange ghosts,' he thought.

11

'Not a witch anywhere,' Perkins thought, and decided to go home.

But which way was home?

He couldn't see anything he knew.

He was **lost!**

12

'Can I help you?'

Perkins blinked. A witch!

13

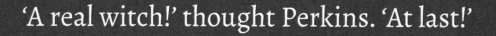

'Agatha Batwing, at your service.'

'A real witch!' thought Perkins. 'At last!'

'Oh no, I'm not a real witch,' Agatha Batwing replied. 'I'm just dressed up as one.'

'So how does she know what I'm thinking?' Perkins thought.

'Lucky guess,' said Agatha.

The not-a-witch stroked Perkins.

'I have room on my broom for a cat.
Would you be interested?'

Perkins looked up
at Agatha Batwing.
She seemed kind.
He was sure she would
look after him.

'But I want to be back in
my basket with my family,'
he thought.

'You're a very wise cat,' said the not-a-witch. 'Are you lost?'

'Yes!'

'You live at 5, Beech Road. That isn't far.'

'Wow! She *is* magic!' thought Perkins.

'Shall I give you a lift home?'

16

It was horrible! Perkins clung on with all his claws.

MAAAAAOOOOOOOWW!

'If it makes you feel better,' said Agatha,
'you're imagining this. I'm not a witch, remember.'

They landed
in the front garden.

Perkins jumped down
and turned to thank Agatha.

But she had vanished.

18

Jessica and Olly were amazed to
see Perkins on the doorstep
when they came home.

When Mum opened the door,
Perkins rushed to his basket
and fell fast asleep.

19

Every Halloween, Perkins sits in the window and thinks about Agatha Batwing flying in the sky, not being a witch.

Then he looks at his cosy basket
and his toys, and thinks,

'How nice to be
a family's cat.'

The End

Word search

Can you find all the Halloween words?

```
h  o  e  r  i  p  m  a  v  t
p  s  w  e  e  t  s  f  a  q
n  u  g  d  y  o  x  c  l  c
d  r  m  i  a  z  b  w  h  o
a  v  g  p  e  r  k  i  n  s
h  j  x  s  k  y  u  t  i  t
t  b  u  f  w  i  p  c  d  u
a  g  h  o  s  t  n  h  g  m
g  n  o  t  e  l  e  k  s  e
a  h  a  l  l  o  w  e  e  n
```

Perkins	costume	Halloween
pumpkin	spider	vampire
witch	sweets	ghost
cat	Agatha	skeleton

Printable version at lizhkidsbooks.wordpress.com

Maze

Can you help Perkins find his way home?

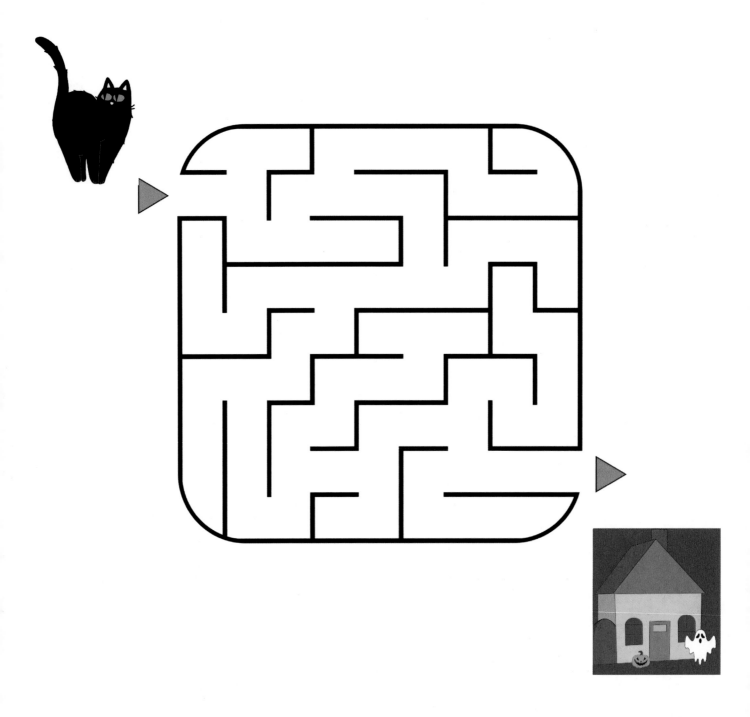

Want more Perkins activities and fun?

Visit lizhkidsbooks.wordpress.com for printable colouring sheets and activities, including some that can be used in class!

Leave a review!

Authors love hearing from their readers!

Please let Liz and Lucy know what you thought of *Perkins the Halloween Cat* by writing a short review on Amazon or your preferred online bookstore. It will help other parents and children find the story.

If you're under 13, please ask a grown-up to help you.

Thank you!

About the Author and Illustrator

Liz Hedgecock usually writes mysteries: some Victorian, some modern. She is owned by two cats, Frankie and Luna.
Perkins the Halloween Cat is her second picture book for children. Why not check out her first, *A Christmas Carrot*?

Terry Crispus hates Christmas: he'd rather keep his presents and dinner for himself. He won't even let his neighbour Mrs Goodenough have a carrot for the reindeer and the snowman's nose.

Then the Christmas Carrot visits Terry at midnight on Christmas Eve and takes him on a host of adventures. Will Terry learn to share before it is too late?

*

Lucy Shaw has just completed a college course in graphic design and photography. Ever since she was little, Lucy had a passion for drawing cartoons and now plans to make a career of it. She has two cute rabbits called Bugs Bunny and Liquorice and a dog called Pixie.

Credits

Maze by platypusmi86 from www.vecteezy.com/free-vector/maze

Fonts: Elsie and Alegreya are both available at fontsquirrel.com (SIL Open Font License v. 1.10).

Made in the USA
Monee, IL
25 October 2022

16539976R00019